Beginning / End

An Esar-Haden Tale

H. Rad Bethlen

Rooster & Raven

For the Daughters of Zeus and Mnemosyne

Author Statement Concerning Artificial Intelligence

The way I write consist of several phases.

1. Idea generation.
2. Research.
3. Story development.
4. Outlining.
5. Writing the rough draft.
6. Editing and rewriting.
7. Editing and polishing.
8. Copy editing.

I will *occasionally* use AI during the research phase if I can't locate some bit of information on my own—but I try to locate it on my own first.

I will *occasionally* use AI during the story's development if I get stuck on something—but I try to resolve my own story issues first.

I *intentionally* use AI during the copy editing phase as a stand-in for a copy editor, which I can't afford to pay for yet which I don't want to go without.

A copy editor is the last set of eyes to look at a manuscript to check for grammar, usage, spelling, and punctuation mistakes. I ask the AI copy editor to make suggestions on corrections. I evaluate those suggestions. If I agree, I make the changes.

I don't use AI for anything else.

Be comforted that this story was written by a human being for other human beings.

H. Rad Bethlen

A delicate perfume overrode the mingled aromas of food, wine, and gutter-stench clouding Ulat-Shen's street-side, open-air stall. It was not a scent Esar-Haden often encountered in the foul-smelling Ghetto of White Skin, a debauched neighborhood in the center of Pwyll, one of the many subterranean cities of the dark elf race.

"Esar-Haden?"

"Nope," he said, not looking up from his food.

"I'm sure of it."

"Got the wrong guy."

She slid onto the adjacent stool. He felt her hand on his thigh. "You fit his description."

He swallowed and looked at her. She was so gorgeous he was stunned. She wore a black cloak, hood up, head bent, but still looking at him. Her long white hair spilled out from the opening, framing her oval face. The front of her cloak was open and he saw she was dressed for a seduction.

"Looking for a lover?" he asked. "I can help, forget that other guy."

She smiled. "That's just what he would say."

"I thought you didn't know him." He turned and picked up a sushi. He wanted to eat them before Ulat-Shen passed by and they disappeared.

"I know everything about you, Esar-Haden. That's why I want to talk to you. I have a business—"

"Got more business than I can handle."

"I know all about that."

He looked at her. "Oh, that's right. You know everything about me."

The thought made him uncomfortable and he started to rise. She rose and slid her arm under his, tugging him into motion. Two men, both dark elves, stepped from the crowd and walked ahead of them, a second pair fell in behind.

Esar-Haden let her pull him along. He was thinking about the most recent spell Soléne had tried to teach him. He struggled to remember the words and how to pronounce them. He was still fumbling over the spell when the group arrived at the mouth of an alley. She pulled him in. The men remained at the entrance. Esar-Haden knew the alley. He knew there was only one way in or out.

"Doorman at Poquelin's Cabaret?" she asked, but it rang like an accusation. "More than a doorman, though. You practically run the place."

"I don't work too hard. Out of curiosity, what's your name? What house are you from?"

"You may call me Seka." She stood so her cloak was open. He couldn't help but admire her dual approach —the body and the muscle, the carrot and the stick. "It's not important what house I belong to, if I even do." She smirked. "From what my sources tell me you take a good percentage of the door."

"Shakedown?"

She chuckled and shook her head. "All that coin and you sleep in a hovel."

"I'm frugal."

"I like you," she said. "You're cute, capable, and creative, but you're undisciplined. You waste all your ill-gotten gains." She frowned. "Aren't much of a long-term thinker, are we?"

"You *really* do know me."

"What you need is a partner." She stepped up and wrapped her arms around his neck, brushing her lips against his. She breathed in his air and gave him hers. "Someone to compensate for your shortcomings. I could do that for you."

"How charitable."

"But that's all in the future." She started to kiss him but pulled back.

"What about now?" he asked.

She gazed up into his eyes. "Now you're going to do me a favor."

. . .

Esar-Haden had to get out of the Ghetto of White Skin. It was all too much. He knew he was being followed. Seka had brought a fifth guy, a guy who knew what he was doing, who had been there the whole time, unseen.

Esar-Haden suspected as much. He figured she was the daughter of a powerful house, not some wannabe, like his own sisters. He knew the Skin. It didn't take long to spot her fifth man—then lose him.

Seka had put some effort into learning about him. He wanted her to understand that she didn't know everything. She had him sleeping in the hovel. That was true, but not every night.

. . .

"Esar!" exclaimed Soléne. "I swear, even though I built that magical portal, it surprises me every time." Soléne was standing in front of a full-length mirror, examining an outfit, a long, thin, black dress with a webbed back. It was little more than lingerie. A pile of rejected clothes was scattered on the bed.

Esar-Haden threw himself down on them.

"Esar! Those are expensive! Shoo! Shoo!" Soléne waved at him.

Esar stood up and walked to an overstuffed chair. He sat on the arm, watching Soléne.

She spun back to the mirror. "What are you doing here?" She looked over her shoulder. "Not that I'm not happy to see you."

"Had to ditch a tail."

Soléne looked at Esar-Haden's reflection in the mirror.

"Nothing to worry about."

"Do I need to turn somebody to stone?" enquired Soléne, still looking at Esar-Haden through the mirror.

"All depends. I might be getting in over my head." He looked into the mirror, into Soléne's large, dark eyes. "You may have to rescue me."

"I *may* have to lock you up and never let you out."

"But then how would I get into trouble?"

"What is it this time? Robbery, smuggling?" She paused, speaking again in a conspiratorial tone. "Assassination?"

"Seating."

"Huh?"

"Seating the right people at the right table. Keeping the wrong people out in the street."

Soléne tossed the outfit, rushed over to Esar-Haden, and leapt into his lap. She wrapped one thin arm around his neck, took up a few strands of her long hair, and began to twirl them. "Tell me everything. You know I love gossip."

. . .

"I'm going with you."

"What?"

"I'm going with you to work tonight," said Soléne, getting up out of his lap.

Esar-Haden sat up. "You hate the Skin."

"I have to find the right outfit," mumbled Soléne.

Esar-Haden frowned.

. . .

"I hate when you sulk," said Soléne.

The pair walked towards the Ghetto of White Skin.

"I don't see—"

8

"I'm a known entity," interrupted Soléne. "People will recognize me."

"But no makeup, those clothes, and you're carrying yourself like—"

"A man?" Soléne chuckled. "Quit being such a baby. We're two males going to the Skin. Nothing unusual about that." Soléne reached out and touched Esar-Haden's cheek. "Let me play in your world for one night."

. . .

"A bit chilling, isn't it?" enquired Erodu, turning away from his simulacrum, a magically created copy of himself. It was without consciousness, otherwise it was an exact, living replica. It lay on a table, covered with a sheet to hide its nudity.

"How does it work?" asked Zai, the matron mother of House Grixx.

"It's quite simple," began Erodu. He turned, looking for somewhere to sit but found nothing. The room was cramped, having just enough space for the table. He turned back to the simulacrum. "Should I become injured, the wounds are transferred to the—" He motioned with his hand to the body breathing under the sheet.

"You remain uninjured?"

"Yes." Erodu smiled. "Amazing what you can do with magic." Erodu smoothed out a wrinkle in his elaborate robe. "There *is* one thing," he looked at Zai. "It doesn't last. The magic unravels, the body decomposes."

"How long?"

"A few days at most. Long enough for what you need, if you act fast. It's a difficult spell. The components are rare and the cost exorbitant. When I came across the spell I was dismayed. It seemed exceedingly useful and nearly impossible to afford, in practical terms." He smiled, "then inspiration struck. You see, I create two. Double the expense, but the usefulness pays for it, and allows for a profit. I leave that with you." He nodded towards the simulacrum. "I'll leave one with House Ah-Trayik. Should one side ambush the other I will no doubt be caught in the fray. The wounds will show up on both copies. Of course, the aggressor won't be surprised. The betrayed house; however, will know at once that their trust has been misplaced." He unconsciously ran a hand over his long beard. "Not to mention, should I personally be insulted with a betrayal of my trust," he looked up into her beautiful, cruel face. "I will exhaust every avenue available to annihilate my newfound enemy."

Matron Mother Zai Grixx smiled, but it was not friendly. "Have you met Matron Mother Rovina Ah-Trayik?"

"I haven't had the pleasure."

"So they don't yet have a simulacrum of you?"

He shook his head.

In a flash of movement Zai reached behind her, slid a dagger out of its sheath, and thrust it into the surprised wizard's neck. She yanked towards her, pulling the blade through the wizard's wind pipe. Where there should have been a fatal wound there was only age-spotted flesh. Zai spun and looked down at the simulacrum.

It convulsed on the table. Gurgling sounds came from the wound as the blood filled its severed airway. Erodu watched in shock as the blood soaked into the once pristine sheet. The body sounded a final sickening gurgle, then lie still.

Zai Grixx reached out and grabbed the wizard's beard, turning his face to hers. "Had to be sure. Lucky for you it works." She glanced to the body, then back to Erodu. "I hope you brought enough of those rare and expensive spell components."

She released his beard and smoothed it. She stepped past him, opened the door, and stepped into the hall. One of her daughters, standing at attention outside of the door, turned to face her. "When our esteemed guest is finished with his fancy spell," said Zai, "show him out, then come back and keep an eye on that thing in there—the," she made air quotes, "living one."

"Yes, Matron Mother."

. . .

Poquelin's Cabaret was full of rowdy men. It was one of the only places in all of Pwyll in which a dark elf male, no matter his station, could be treated well. In Poquelin's he could be the master of his domain—until his coin purse had been emptied.

There were plenty of women in the large room; women of all types and races from the surface. They sat in laps, flirted, kissed, teased, and whispered their knowledge and enthusiasm for the carnal pleasures into pointed, ebony ears. Their talents were in feeding the male ego.

Women with still more talent could be found on stage, singing, dancing, performing ribald skits, and reciting the poetry of love and lust. Many of these women were also skilled in the art of lovemaking and could be had —for a price.

Esar-Haden's keen eyes saw every interaction. He made it his business to intervene in every romance, to ensure the right amount of coin was exchanged, and that the secretive owners of Poquelin's Cabaret got their cut.

He shut the front door and looked up into the face of a gnoll, a seven foot tall half-human, half-hyena named Kiula. "No one else but regulars, understand?" Kiula curled back her lips, revealing black and pink spotted gums and gleaming white fangs. "I don't care how much coin they stuff in your paw, or how many threats they utter. I'm serious. If you don't recognize them, tell them to —" He smiled and winked.

He reached into his jacket and produced a large emerald. He let it flash in the light from the chandeliers. Kiula glanced down at it. She looked back to Esar-Haden. She reached down and ran the tip of her thumb over the exposed blade of her battle axe. Esar-Haden tossed the gem. Kiula deftly plucked it from the air. "If you think you need more of a bribe than that, you're worse than a dark elf," muttered Esar-Haden, turning away from the gnoll.

He glanced at a table at the rear. A lone "male" sat, hidden in an oversized cloak. A pair of glasses and a bottle of red wine sat on the table. He looked to a large semi-circular table at the front of the stage. Two males sat on one side, two on the other side. In between them sat a male from the surface—a wizard in elaborate robes.

Clinging to his arm was a surface woman, one the wizard had brought with him. She was dressed as elaborately and as richly as he was. She wore a pale yellow dress, her blonde hair held in place with diamond-studded pins, and was clearly highborn. Her skin and teeth were too perfect to be anything less than noble in birth.

Esar-Haden suspected the wizard had offered to take her on a trip to the fabled and dangerous city of the dark elves. She would, he no doubt promised, be absolutely safe, so long as she stayed by his side.

She was also pregnant. It wasn't obvious. She wasn't too far along and the dress hid her growing middle. But Esar-Haden had pulled her chair for her. He noticed how she reached for her stomach when she sat. He wondered if it was the wizard's. Bringing his pregnant bride to Pwyll was an idiotic idea.

He knew that no matter how powerful one was, there was always someone or something more dangerous out there. He also knew, from long experience, that when one got involved in house politics one had to take every precaution. The wizard, it seemed, was too arrogant to bother.

Esar-Haden looked to Orm, the black-bearded dwarf behind the bar, and nodded. Orm nodded back, stepped over to a rope-pull, and yanked twice. Esar-Haden knew a bell was ringing back stage. He made his way through the crowd until he reached the small, high table at the back. He sat and glanced at Soléne.

"How long do we have to wait?" she whispered.

"Not long," grumbled Esar-Haden.

"Oh, cheer up," chastised Soléne. "Aren't we having fun?"

Esar-Haden scowled.

"Is that your 'I'm serious' work face?" she asked, reaching under the table to pinch his inner thigh.

"I hate you," he mumbled.

"Such a drama queen," joked Soléne. "That's them, isn't it? No house markings."

"I went to the military academy with one of them."

"What house is he from?"

"Hell if I remember," admitted Esar-Haden.

A dark elf male parted the black velvet curtains and stepped out. His costume was that of a surface wizard; black robes with arcane symbols stitched in silver thread, his shoulders covered with raven feathers, a long, twisted wooden staff held in one hand. When he saw an actual surface wizard sitting at his feet, he bowed. He rose and began his spiel.

Esar had heard it many times. He bent and was about to whisper in Soléne's ear when he noticed a pair of eyes that were not on the presenter, but on him. The male sat by himself, near the corner of the room, scowling at Esar-Haden. It took him a moment to recognize the fifth of Seka's men, the professional among them.

'How did he get in here,' he asked himself.

"—necromancer or transmutationist."

"Huh?"

"Haven't you been listening?" asked Soléne.

"No."

"I think he's a necromancer or a transmutationist."

"You can tell that just by looking?"

"His robes, silly. He has symbols from those two schools stitched into his robes. Protection spells, I imagine. Rather obvious, but perhaps that's the point."

"Should I be worried?"

"Are you going to attack him?"

"Hadn't planned on it."

"Then don't worry." Soléne took a drink of wine. "They aren't well known symbols. He's no novice." She looked to Esar-Haden. "You remember yet what house he's from?" She nodded to the male dark elf Esar-Haden had recognized.

"I didn't know I was supposed to be remembering that."

"Esar-Haden, if I have to piece all of this together for you I'm going to want a cut of your gold."

"Speaking of—" said Esar. He saw a man reaching into his coin purse. The woman in his lap was smiling and holding out her hand. He rose from the table and made his way over to the eager couple.

. . .

"You follow those two," whispered Soléne. "I'll follow those two."

Esar-Haden, Soléne, and the gnoll stood at the front door.

"Haven't you had enough fun?" asked Esar.

"You need my help."

"You're going to get yourself hurt," he warned. "It's two on one and you don't even have a weapon."

"Oh, silly boy."

"What about the wizard?" asked Esar-Haden. "Who'll follow him?"

"No need. He'll stay in the Skin. The nicest place he can find. Hurry, Esar, they're getting away." Soléne darted through the door and fell in behind the pair of dark elves.

"Lock up, will ya?" he called out to Orm. "I guess my night's just getting started." The dwarf nodded. Esar-Haden exited the cabaret.

He began to follow the other pair of males. The duo made a few other stops in the Ghetto of White Skin. They darted through a alleys and meandered their way from neighborhood to neighborhood. 'Working awfully hard to lose any tails,' thought Esar-Haden, as he once again dodged out of sight. 'I guarantee the others have shaken Soléne by now.'

. . .

Soléne had learned what she wanted to learn, and was taking a round-about way back home. She was feeling rather self-congratulatory when an arm shot from the darkness, a hand wrapped around her throat. It was Seka's fifth man. A dagger flashed and was held with the point just below her jaw.

"Who are you?" he whispered.

Soléne closed her eyes and concentrated. The male wasn't choking her, merely holding her. He was standing behind her, hiding himself. This meant he couldn't see her lips. Soléne began to whisper the words of a spell. She traced unnatural shapes with her fingers. The man didn't notice.

"A buddy of Esar-Haden's?" he asked. "Whatever angle you two are working it ain't worth it. This thing's bigger than either of you. I promise, you ain't getting paid enough. Tell me what you know and we can work this out."

Soléne's voice rose above a whisper as the final words of the spell passed her lips.

"What's that?" asked her assailant.

"Just a little spell."

"What?" asked the male, digging the tip of his dagger into Soléne's flesh. The cut was slight, but Soléne relished the note of pain. She felt the line of blood run down her neck.

The man watched with surprise as the long, white hair of his captive began to float. He tried to press the dagger in deeper, to squeeze Soléne's neck tighter, but the hair snaked around his wrists and took control of his actions. The magicked hair pulled his arms out wide. He struggled to break free but couldn't. He tried to yell but hair wrapped around his throat and constricted, silencing him.

Soléne turned to face her attacker. She was surrounded by a crown of "living" hair. Some coiled like a serpent ready to strike. The rest bound the man. Soléne looked to the dagger. With a mental command her hair shook the man's wrist. The dagger clattered to the ground.

Soléne's hair wrapped around the man's face, covering his nose and mouth, leaving an opening for his eyes. Still more hair snaked around his throat. With a thought the magicked hair constricted. The man began to convulse as his lungs struggled to draw air. Soléne watched as panic and fear flashed in the man's eyes. The pair stood in silence as his life was pulled from him by the "living" hair.

Soléne commanded her hair to release her attacker. His corpse crumpled at her feet. She knelt and looked into his lifeless eyes. *"Now* I've had enough fun." She rose, turned, and made her way home.

. . .

"House Ah-Trayik," concluded Soléne.

"The other?"

"Not sure, yet," admitted Soléne. "Whichever house it is, they're being careful."

"What's up with the dried blood on your neck?"

"Hold me, Esar."

"I *am* holding you."

"Hold me tighter."

. . .

Esar-Haden sat on a stone bench that was umbrellaed by a giant gold-green mushroom. He hated that they, House Koi Ki, who "controlled" the Ghetto of White Skin, let these enormous, stupid looking mushrooms grow in the filth and rotting refuse that was swept into the gutters by the street merchants. Every time he saw one he wanted to cut it down but he had heard that Matron Mother Taschen herself liked them, saying they added charm to an otherwise ugly section of town.

The dark elf rogue glanced from the fleshy gills above him to a pair of fleshy, bare legs belonging to one of the surface females brought into the caves of Pwyll to entertain, by choice or force, the restless dark elves. She passed out of view. He returned his attention to the food stall across the street. A pair of large eyes set atop a frog-like head could be seen glancing over the heads of those sitting at the counter.

A customer pushed his bowl and cup away from him then reached into his jacket for his money pouch. He tossed a few copper coins onto the counter. Ulat-Shen reached over the heads of his seated customers and extended his long, webbed fingers, careful not to let his forearm fin hit anyone. He waved Esar-Haden over.

"Sweet beans and sushi—two."

"Two!" cried Ulat-Shen. "Do you know how hard it is to get fish through the desert above, down here into these miserable caves, and keep it fresh? It cost a fortune! You want two?"

"How about three?" asked Esar-Haden. "Two for me and one for you." He reached into a pocket and tossed a pair of gold coins onto the counter. "And don't lie. I know you get your fish from an underground lake."

"You know a lot. You big-time-operator now, huh?" asked Ulat-Shen. He swept the coins off of the counter, into his apron pocket. He spun and began to prepare Esar-Haden's sushi.

"And wine," added Esar-Haden.

Ulat-Shen's assistant, a goblin, small, green-skinned, and stupid, stepped up onto the box behind the counter and placed a ceramic cup in front of the dark elf. Even with the assistance of the box the goblin was barely tall enough to reach the counter. Esar-Haden could only make out the goblin's large, dull eyes, and his long, pointed nose, which drug along the counter, leaving a trail of snot.

The goblin giggled as he poured the steaming wine into the cup and waited. Esar-Haden eyed him. He didn't like the giggle. He downed the contents in one gulp and set the cup back. The goblin refilled it, spilling wine on his own nose, and giggled at whatever mystery he alone knew then descended out of sight.

Ulat-Shen turned and set a small plate and a shallow bowl in front of Esar-Haden. The bowl held a pile of heavily seasoned, bright-green beans. The plate held three rectangles of tofu with a sliver of orange fish atop them all wrapped in what appeared to be dark-green seaweed. Before Esar-Haden could make a move, Ulat-Shen produced a pair of chopsticks and plucked one of the sushi from the plate. He deftly popped it into his mouth. He half bowed to Esar-Haden, his head fin waving. When he stood back up his eyes settled on something or someone behind his customer.

Esar-Haden glanced over his shoulder.

"I'm mad at you," said Seka.

"I thought things went well."

"Eat fast."

. . .

Seka led Esar-Haden by the arm. This time they didn't go to the alley, but to his one-room hovel. He noticed she wasn't dressed for a seduction, but for the possibility of combat. He guessed the honeymoon was over. As they approached the door a dark elf male stepped out.

"It's safe," he said to Seka. He sneered at Esar-Haden.

She led him through the doorway. Esar-Haden noted the lock had been busted. She pushed him into the small room and shut the door. He turned to face her. She advanced and pushed him backwards onto the bed. He fell onto his butt, his back against the wall.

She lifted her leg and placed one stiletto-heeled boot between his legs. Esar-Haden looked up at her and tried to discern her mood. She helped him by smiling. "My faith in you was well placed," she said, bending forward to rest her elbow on her knee, chin on her fist. "The first meeting went just as I'd hoped."

"And that made you mad?"

"I know."

"Know what?"

"You ditched him once, was it too much trouble to ditch him twice? Good help is hard to find." The blank look in Esar-Haden's face made her curious. "You have no idea what I'm talking about, do you?" Esar-Haden shook his head. "You didn't kill him?"

Esar-Haden pieced everything together. Seka's man must have followed Soléne. He wondered if Soléne had killed him, she hadn't mentioned it. Then again, she was in an unusual mood last night, and there was the cut on her neck.

"I didn't kill your guy."

"Well," said Seka. "That worries me. Now I have to find out who *did* kill him and why?"

"It's a dangerous city."

She chuckled at his observation. "I want you to secure a private place for a second meeting," she said. "Private, understand? Make sure it can seat four people."

"A few places come to mind."

"Don't tell anyone." She lifted her foot from the bed and stood. She produced a pouch from the folds of her cloak and tossed it on the mattress. He heard the jingle of coin. "Privacy is everything. I'm going to be attending this meeting myself."

. . .

"You can't be serious," complained Seka. "Your hovel?" She looked at him. "There isn't even enough room."

"I cleared everything out and borrowed four chairs." Seka began to protest. Esar-Haden cut her off. "Look." He nodded to one end of the narrow alley. Seka frowned at being silenced, but looked. It took her a moment to pick out the crouching form of a gnoll, partially hidden by a massive stalagmite. "There," Esar nodded to the other end of the alley. Seka followed his eyes to Orm, standing in the middle of the alleyway's entrance, propping himself up on a war hammer that was nearly as tall as he was. "All cordoned off. No front doors open into this alley. I may live in the ghetto, but I live smart."

Seka nodded to one of her men. He left the alley. She looked at Esar-Haden, shook her head, and stepped into his back-alley shack. Esar-Haden followed. Before too long the door opened and an unknown male stepped into the room. He looked at both Esar-Haden and Seka. He leaned out of the doorway and spoke to someone outside. He stepped back into the room and sat in the empty chair across from Esar-Haden. A female dark elf stepped into the room. She eyed Esar-Haden and Seka with obvious distain. One of Seka's men shut the door.

'Soléne was right,' mused Esar-Haden, 'Anna Ah-Trayik.' He averted his gaze, as was expected of a male.

"What's this!" hissed the eldest daughter of House Ah-Trayik. "Where is Zai Grixx?"

'Grixx!' Thought Esar-Haden. He looked sidelong at Seka. Perspiration beaded on her forehead at the mention of the name. She looked at him. Their eyes met. He read her thoughts. 'She screwed up inviting me to this.' He controlled his demeanor, looking nonplused. He even went so far as to examine the dirt beneath his fingernails.

Anna Ah-Trayik turned towards the door.

"My matron mother," Seka stood as she spoke, "is cautious, but serious."

'I certainly am learning a lot,' thought Esar-Haden.

Anna turned and looked at Seka. The hovel was so tight the two women stood breasts-to-breasts. The mood in the room was tense.

Esar-Haden looked to the other male. He had his hand on the hilt of his sword, looking at Seka. Esar-Haden smiled. He knew the room was too tight for the man to draw and effectively use a blade that long. Esar-Haden slid out one of his daggers and held it at the side of his thigh.

"I am Seka Grixx. I speak for my matron mother, with her permission." She sat down.

Anna glared at Seka. "Never heard of you. I know all the daughters of House Grixx."

Seka looked sidelong at Esar-Haden yet again. She looked to Anna. "I'm an Alamuti Ascetic. I was taken to their monastery at birth."

'Well damn,' thought Esar-Haden.

"Grixx has an ascetic?" Anna studied Seka. The revelation had reduced her arrogance by half. "Your house is full of surprises." She sat. She leaned her head to her male bodyguard. "I should have brought fifty males." She smiled. "That is if she really is an ascetic, or even a daughter of House Grixx."

"If this was a trap, you'd be dead already," observed Esar-Haden. He sheathed his dagger with a sigh of defeated resignation.

Anna turned sharply to him. "How dare you address me!"

Esar-Haden looked at her. He was in no mood for proper etiquette. He wasn't even sure he was going to leave the meeting alive. 'I know too much now because of your big mouth,' he thought. 'If only you'd had some tact.' He condemned her, silently. Still, despite his change of mood, he regretted his outburst.

"Despite the male's," Seka looked from Anna to Esar, then back to Anna, "insolence, may I remind you, we have much more important matters to discuss."

"About time," muttered Anna, looking away from Esar-Haden.

"Our houses have been warring for a generation," continued Seka. "We've wasted our energies tearing each other down for too long. Meanwhile our common foe," she glanced at Esar-Haden, "grows more powerful." She looked back at her hoped-for ally. "If our houses continue along this path for another generation we'll leave nothing for our mutual enemy to destroy." Anna nodded in agreement. Seka continued. "Matron Mother Grixx feels that our houses should combine forces."

A sinister smile spread across Anna's face. "The enemy of my enemy is my friend."

"We have been at war for so long few would suspect us of uniting against a third."

"Zai certainly is clever," stated Anna.

"She's smart. This is the smart thing to do."

"She's paranoid," argued Anna. "More than most dark elves." She eyed Seka. "An ascetic *and* a surface wizard. She's taking every precaution."

"Matron Mother Zai wants the final meeting to go well. There's a great deal at stake."

"Zai fears an attempt on her life?" Anna chuckled. "House Ah-Trayik fears nothing and no one," she boasted. "We may be smaller than Grixx but we've fought you to a standstill for years."

Seka ignored the jab. "That must come to an end."

Anna smiled. "After a generation of war a daughter of House Ah-Trayik and a daughter of House Grixx have met without bloodshed." She laughed. "All according to Zai's plan. Set the third meeting. I hope Zai recognizes the patience Matron Mother Rovina shows by allowing her to control things at this early stage. It won't be that way for long." Anna looked around the hovel, smirking. She stood, as did her bodyguard.

"The matron mother of House Grixx sends her regards to your matron mother," said Seka, also rising. Esar-Haden rose. Seka and the male had their backs to him. Anna was facing Seka, ignoring the male who had dared violate her authority. Anna looked into the face of her rival, for they were still rivals until the matron mothers of both houses met.

"Together we will destroy House Isuph," said Anna Ah-Trayik.

Esar-Haden was glad no one saw the look of shock on his face. 'House Isuph!' he thought. 'Soléne!'

Anna Ay-Trayik and her bodyguard left the hovel. Seka stood in the doorway watching them pass out of the alley. She slammed the door and spun on Esar-Haden. "What was that!" she screamed. She grabbed his jacket and pushed him backwards until he slammed into the wall. The flimsy boards shook. "You couldn't keep your mouth shut for five minutes?"

"It was her," Esar-Haden nodded towards the chair in which Anna Ay-Trayik had sat, "who couldn't keep *her* mouth shut."

"If she had demanded your death I would have given it to her."

"And here I thought we were starting to trust one another."

Seka yanked him from the wall and slammed him back into it. She released him and plopped down into a chair. She bent forward and placed her elbows on her knees. "It's my fault," she admitted. She glanced at Esar-Haden. "You should have been outside, with the others." She sat up. "Truth is, I was scared. I didn't want to be in here alone with them. They could have killed me. Zai is taking a huge risk. House Ah-Trayik could use this as an opportunity to betray us and turn the tide of battle their way." She looked at Esar-Haden, who had not even bothered to straighten his jacket. "Surprised at my honesty?"

"Surprised at your worry. I thought Alamuti Ascetics were fearless." He pushed himself from the wall and pulled down the hem of his jacket.

Seka scoffed. "You believed that lie?" She shook her head. "An ascetic would never rely on a rogue male." She laughed. "They wouldn't need to." She looked at him. "You should know that."

Esar-Haden sat down across from her. He was about to speak but Seka anticipated his question.

"I'm not a daughter of House Grixx. I'm a hired hand, just like you. Expendable, just like you." She smiled at Esar-Haden. "You're really in a fix now." She reached out and patted his knee. "Don't worry. I'm not going to kill you."

"Thanks."

"I can't let you out of my sight until this is all over."

"Until the third meeting is over or until House Isuph is over?" He thought of Soléne. House Isuph had been dominant for so long that it was difficult to imagine it any other way. 'You've certainly led a charmed life,' Esar thought of his lover. 'If your house had been at war all these years you would have not been allowed to satisfy your lust with a low-born male.' The line of thought was depressing.

He looked at Seka. She seemed to be pondering the answer to his question. He wondered, though, if he cared enough to risk his life for Soléne. He had always gone his own way, a loner, looking out for himself. 'Would she risk her life for me,' he asked himself. 'A gutter rat? A lover she sneaks in and out of her chambers?' He was careful not to frown. 'Does she care, or am I merely entertaining her?' That line of thought was as depressing as the first. He gave it up for the time being. 'House Grixx.' He looked away from Seka. He glanced to the empty chair next to him, picturing its most recent occupant, 'House Ay-Trayik.' He worked hard to hide his consternation and worry from the female across from him. 'Damn it, Esar, what are you going to do?'

"I thought this was easy money," he muttered.

"No such thing," muttered Seka.

. . .

Now wearing a dress of light blue with touches of gold thread, Princess Daphnia roamed the open bazaar.

She eyed the bodyguard hired by Erodu. "You annoy me," she stated. He looked at her but did not reply. "You stand too close and you're hideous." She turned over an expertly crafted hair pin. It was silver with gold inlay. She was reminded of one of the suitors her father had tempted her with. "Tall and thin, he looks like a pin!" She repeated the insult she had turned the suitor away with and tossed the pin back into the wooden case from which she had plucked it. She turned to the male dark elf. "Can't you stand up straight?"

"An old wound, Mistress."

"You're bent like a piece of greenwood, dried behind the stove." She laughed. "That's what I'll call you, Greenwood the Ugly." She smirked, enjoying her own humor. She glanced from him to the crowded street. She decided Pwyll, for all its exotic charm, was beneath her. She regretted coming. Still, she hated to be away from Erodu, now that she carried his son. She was certain it was a son. 'My father tried every suitor,' she thought. 'I chose my own.' She looked back to the male. 'Look how weak and pathetic he is. Not like my Erodu. He could bring this whole city down.'

"Manners, manners. Remember you're a guest here."

Princess Daphnia turned to the speaker. A female dark elf stood too close. Daphnia looked to her bodyguard, he was gone. Two males she didn't recognize stood in his place. She looked back to the female dark elf.

"I'm Princess—"

"I know who you are," interrupted the female from House Grixx.

"Leave me alone," warned Daphnia, her voice wavering. "My husband is Erodu the Great, High Wizard of—"

The female dark elf slid a dagger from the sheath at her belt, silencing the princess. The blade glinted in the magical floating globes illuminating the bazaar. Daphnia looked at it, stunned. "I can't be touched," she whispered. "He said I can't be touched."

The female from House Grixx reached out and took the surface woman's arm. She pulled her into motion. The tip of her dagger found its way to Daphnia's side, passed through the blue and gold fabric, and bit into her skin, but not deep enough to hurt her.

"Is it true you're pregnant?" she asked, her voice smoother than the surface of the discarded hair pin.

. . .

"You're brilliant, sadistic, but brilliant," whispered Seka as she bent next to Esar-Haden, undressing, as was he. "Look how pissed off everyone is."

Esar-Haden looked around the cave. It was longer than it was wide with only one way in. The cave was filled with steaming water, a hot spring. Only a narrow edge of stone allowed one to skirt the pool. The spring itself was shaped like the number eight. 'For once my time at the military academy paid off,' he thought.

The hot spring, a healthy distance from the main caves of Pwyll, was a favorite hideout for the cadets of the military academy. They could sneak away from their instructors, absconding with a couple of bottles of wine, and relax in the hot water, releasing the stress in their bruised and battered bodies.

He knew that the matron mothers of House Ay-Trayik and House Grixx would be unfamiliar with the hot spring, which made it an ideal location. Neither house wanted the other to have an advantage. He glanced at Seka. 'Not even she'd heard of it.'

Seka had been reluctant to leave the city in order to scout the site, despite his reassurances. Since the second meeting she had been on edge and paranoid. She knew her mistake, inviting him to the second meeting resulted in a threat to his life. She suspected he wanted to escape her control. She was right, but not entirely for the right reasons.

As they had scoured the city, Esar-Haden looked for any opportunity to ditch Seka and her henchmen, all to no avail. He needed to warn Soléne, while something could be done, when the alliance against her house could actually be stopped. Seka's extreme paranoia and watchful eye, not to mention the constant presence of her henchmen, had made escape impossible.

He glanced at Seka's pile of clothing. She had sent her henchmen back to Pwyll, ostensibly to make all parties concerned more comfortable. Esar-Haden frowned. Now was his opportunity to escape, but it was too late. He doubted he could make it all the way to Soléne to warn her. It didn't matter. He had already accepted his fate.

He noticed that Anna Ay-Trayik was staring at him, her face twisted in anger. She was reluctantly undressing. The very idea of holding the secret meeting at a hot spring, all parties required to skinny dip, was incredibly insulting. It was also desirable. With all parties vulnerable, the power dynamic had been equalized. Anna caught the attention of her matron mother.

Rovina Ay-Trayik stood in perfect nudity. Her hair was held up by some elaborate, glittering piece of jewelry. Other than that she was bare. A male stood next to her, also naked, holding mother and daughter's clothing and weapons, as well as his own. At her daughter's direction Matron Mother Rovina looked to Esar-Haden. Her bearing was regal, commanding, and intimidating, despite her nudity. She smiled at Esar-Haden and nodded. She found his selection amusing.

"Where's Zai?" growled Anna Ah-Trayik.

Seka walked to the cave's entrance. "I directed them to take the longer route here." She looked from the tunnel to Anna. "I thought it would be poor form to have you all bump into each other in the tunnels leading here."

Matron Mother Rovina chuckled but didn't acknowledge the speaker. She eased herself into the pool. Anna followed. Their male attendants began to carefully arrange the group's combined weapons and clothing on the slippery ledge of stone.

It had been decided that the males, Esar-Haden included, were to occupy the pool nearest the cave's entrance. The surface wizard was excluded from this. He was going to sit between the matron mothers, fulfilling his duties as negotiator and safeguard against betrayal.

The wizard had protested the loudest to the hot spring. Esar-Haden knew why. The protective spells stitched into his robes meant little if he wasn't wearing them. The wizard, still complaining, lowered his aged, naked body into the water. Finding the temperature agreeable he submersed himself to the chin, his beard floating, and began to maneuver between the pools. His mood changed. He reminded himself that he was invulnerable for the time being thanks to his twin simulacrums. He rolled onto his back and floated.

. . .

Matron Mother Zai Grixx stood alone in the cramped room, having sent her daughter out in the hall to wait for her command. Elsewhere in House Grixx her males were armed and ready for battle. Zai Grixx stared down at the wizard's simulacrum. She reached out, grabbed the edge of the blanket, and threw it from the body. She ran her hand just above the breathing but silent mass, feeling its warmth. She wanted to smile, but would wait.

. . .

Esar-Haden glanced around the cave. Seka was still at the entrance, peering down the tunnel that led back to Pwyll. Daughter and mother were conversing. The males were wading into the water. The wizard floated on his back, studying the contours of the cave's ceiling and the twin magical orbs that lit the small space. For the moment no eyes were on Esar-Haden. He knew it was time but hesitated. He was hung up on how this all ended—with him dead. It made him a little sad.

'Despite all your grumbling,' he told himself, 'you actually enjoy life.' He frowned. 'Will she even know?' He wondered if and how Soléne would learn of his final heroic act. 'I would have never guessed—a martyr to love.' He realized he was staring at the wizard's water-speckled beard. He shook his head clear and took a deep breath. He made once last sweep of the room with his eyes then knelt and grabbed the handles of his daggers.

He glanced at Seka. She turned and was watching him. The look on her face was not what he expected, but he didn't have time to think about it. He stood, flipped the daggers in the air and caught them by the tips. He launched himself into the air, and lifted his legs, compacting his body into a tight ball.

His activity drew the attention of everyone in the pool. He lifted his arms above his head. The two males began to turn in the water, thinking about their weapons. Anna Ah-Trayik began to move as well, trying to get between the airborne male, his daggers, and her mother. The wizard, seeing something quite unexpected in the air above him, started to right himself. Rovina Ah-Trayik did not lose, not even for an instant, her regal bearing. Her dark eyes watched Esar-Haden as if his actions had nothing to do with her.

Esar brought his arms down, throwing first one dagger, then the other. The gleaming streaks of silver crossed the space. Their reflections danced on the surface of the spring. The first dagger hit Anna Ah-Trayik in the chest. The second dagger, having glided along a separate but similar path, struck Rovina Ah-Trayik in the divot at the base of her throat.

Esar-Haden thrust his legs down with all the strength he could muster. One of his heels struck the wizard on the bridge of his nose, the other on his corner of his cheek bone. Having overshot the wizard, Esar dropped into the pool just in front of him. He reached up and behind him, attempting to grab the wizard. His fingers grasped at air. His head went beneath the water.

He kept himself submerged, swimming forward, eyes open. He wanted to get away from the wizard, or get to his daggers, he wasn't sure. He wasn't thinking, but operating on battle instinct. As he swam, Rovina Ah-Trayik sunk beneath the surface. Her face was as perfectly composed as a statue's, and equally as lifeless. A pair of arms reached into the water, grabbing for her. She slipped through them.

A pair of arms reached for Esar-Haden and caught him. He was pulled to the surface. One of the males had him. Esar lifted his feet, placed them against the male's chest, and thrust. The two flew apart. Esar went back under the water.

He came back up in the center of the pool. Anna Ah-Trayik was behind him, clutching her chest, glassy-eyed, paused in the act of climbing onto the thin ledge of stone. Her breathing was loud, ragged. A vivid line of blood ran down from the dagger between her breasts. Esar spun, anticipating threats from the other direction. What he saw surprised him. Seka was airborne. The males had turned their attention from him to the new arrival. The wizard was attempting to concentrate on a spell.

Judging from Seka's arc she was intent on interrupting the wizard. This threw Esar off. He paused, unsure. He had expected Seka to come for him, along with the males, and the wizard. Seka turned her head to the side. Her shoulder struck the wizard in the back of his neck. Her momentum carried both of them under the water. The water of the spring was turning red.

. . .

The wizard's simulacrum jerked. Water began to spill from its parted lips and flow from its nostrils. Zai Grixx smiled. She placed her hand on the grey-haired chest. The body convulsed beneath her touch. "He's drowning."

Her curiosity begged to know what exactly was happening at the third and final meeting. She hoped Seka would survive to tell her. She turned from the dying simulacrum, walked to the door, and opened it. Her daughter turned to face her.

"Begin the attack," commanded Zai. She glanced back at the simulacrum, watched its final tortured convulsions, then shut the door.

. . .

"Tell me again, Esar," begged Soléne. She wrapped her arms around her lover.

"I'm sleepy."

"I know, I just want to hear it again." Soléne lifted her face to Esar-Haden's and kissed him. She pulled back and looked into his eyes. "My savior. I'm surprised."

"You already said that."

"I am, though." Soléne studied her lover's face. "I never thought you would risk your life for me. It's *too* romantic."

"I didn't know I would either."

Soléne propped herself up on her elbow. "Seka certainly fooled you. She really did know everything about you, about *us*." Soléne pursed her lips. "I guess we aren't as much of a secret as I thought. Zai Grixx knows. I wonder who else? She certainly didn't waste the knowledge."

"She took a hell of a gamble."

"You think?" asked Solène.

"How did she know I would do it, go after Rovina?"

"Well," Soléne thought. "Either you would or you wouldn't. If you did, you would either succeed," she smiled at her lover, "or fail. If you succeeded, she gets what she wanted, Rovina Ah-Trayik dead. If you failed, so what? She would reveal our secret and blame my house. Claiming Seka had been betrayed by you; which, technically she was. Sure, Ah-Trayik would be angry, the truce would be off, but Zai wouldn't be making a new enemy, just keeping an old one. I don't see a downside for her. It's quite a brilliant plan. I'm impressed. If only I could get to know Zai better. I could learn from her."

"Better not."

"Oh?"

"She's going to turn that strategic mind to your house next. Are you worried?"

"Nah, it will take her years to rebuild her strength. She has to keep a low profile for a bit. Despite the success of her little plot, House Ah-Trayik went down fighting. I heard she suffered significant losses assaulting their compound."

"Maybe she's vulnerable. Your house going to attack?"

Soléne shrugged a shoulder. "Not for me to decide."

"Ah, well, I'll rest easy for a night, then. I've earned it," said Esar-Haden. He lifted his arms and placed his hands behind his head.

"So Seka didn't kill you, huh?" asked Soléne.

"She let me walk away."

"She didn't want to tie up loose ends?"

"We have an understanding," said Esar, winking.

"Birds of a feather?"

"Something like that."

"Remind me about the wizard," said Soléne. "He didn't drown?"

"Somehow not," said Esar-Haden. "Seka held him under long enough that he should have."

"Maybe a water breathing spell," said Soléne. "Or something else. Transmutation is an amazing school of magic. So why didn't he kill all of you?"

"The princess."

Soléne looked at Esar.

"Zai was holding her hostage. Seka informed him —when he came up for air."

"He gave a damn about *her*?" asked Soléne.

"She's pregnant with his child," said Esar-Haden. "Didn't you notice?"

"No." Soléne rest her head on Esar-Haden's chest. "Tell me again, from the beginning."

H. Rad Bethlen has been compared to Isak Dinesen (*Seven Gothic Tales*) and Fritz Leiber (*Swords and Deviltry*). He is known for his work in the fantasy and horror genres as well as his non-fiction. He has been published in Europe and America.

Enjoy the story?

If you liked what you read, please take a moment to **leave a review on Amazon**! Your feedback helps other readers find this story. It only takes a minute but it makes a huge difference. The Amazon algorithm requires 30-50 reviews before it will pick this book up and promote it to like-minded readers. Your review is instrumental in helping that happen!

For more great fiction and non-fiction please visit:

roosterandravenpublishing.com

hradbethlen.com

or H. Rad Bethlen's Amazon page.